Paul Jewett, William Barrett

The New-England Farrier

A Compendium of Earriery

Paul Jewett, William Barrett

The New-England Farrier
A Compendium of Earriery

ISBN/EAN: 9783337330071

Printed in Europe, USA, Canada, Australia, Japan

Cover: Foto ©Andreas Hilbeck / pixelio.de

More available books at **www.hansebooks.com**

New-England Farrier;

or,

A COMPENDIUM OF FARRIERY,

IN FOUR PARTS:

Wherein moft of the Difeafes to which Horfes, Neat Cattle, Sheep and Swine are incident, are treated of; with Medical and Surgical obfervations thereon.

The Remedies, in general, are fuch as are eafily procured, fafely applied, and happily fuccefsful ; being the refult of many years experience—and firft production of the kind in *New-England.*

INTENDED FOR THE USE OF

Private Gentlemen and Farmers.

By PAUL JEWETT,

OF ROWLEY.

NEWBURYPORT—PRINTED

By WILLIAM BARRETT,

At his PRINTING-OFFICE Merrimack-Street.

MDCCXCV.

INTRODUCTION.

THE fubfequent treatife owes its rife to three principal caufes.

I. The great opportunity I had, whilft young, of reading authors on Farriery, and thereby gaining an extenfive theory.

II. The extenfive practice I have had in this kind of bufinefs fince, and the reafons experience hath given me, to differ from moft of the European theories, and confine my practice to obfervation only.

III. The folicitations of my acquaintance.

In a work of this kind, I cannot be fo particular in my prefcriptions for cures as I am in my daily practice: The conftitutions of beafts being different, will require fome difference in the treatment, which muft be directed by the judgment of thofe who are prefent.

I SHALL, in the firft place, make fome remarks on the choice of feed horfes, and treatment of horfes in general. On the management of colts till three years old, and at firft riding them. Directions for docking, nicking, &c.— Likewife, of the various maladies with which they are affected.

Secondly, I fhall treat of the various difeafes affecting Neat Cattle. Sheep and Swine, in the next place, will claim our attention.

PART

Of SEED HORSES, *and the management of* COLTS.

SUCH feed horfes fhould be chofen as are large and well proportioned, ftrait limbed, moving in a right line, heedlefs of every thwarting object, of an even perfevering temper, with fhort fine hair and lively countenance.

Colts, when they are foaled, require but little attention the firft three or four months. When they are weaned (if by grafs) they fhould be kept in a fmall inclofure, with a conftant fupply of water, and tender herbage : If they are weaned by hay, provide yourfelf with a quantity of rowin or fecond crop hay ; which is a grateful fodder for their tender years, and eafily mafticated ; while coarfe hay would be neglected, and your colt ftarved.

Colts of the firft and fecond year, are frequently troubled with the lampers, being a flefhy excrefence, or fpongy fubftance, growing in the roof of the mouth, and hindering the colt from chewing. The beft method of curing this inconvenience is, by applying a hot iron with a round head, till it is burnt fo as to flough off ; and in a few days it is well.

Give your colt a good pafture till he is three or four years old. then you muft apply your rules of inftruction to form the horfe's manners ; for your horfe therefore often, and but little at a time; let his water alfo be given him when he crav-s; fome horfes are more thirfty than others, and unlefs indulged with water will refufe the choiceft hay. There is likewife a great choice in water. Thofe waters that readily mix with alkalin fubftances and common foap, are beft fuited to dilute the food, and promote the fecretions of an animal body.

ON EXERCISE.

A HORSE that hath been ufed to labour, or fuffered to roam abroad, is an unfuitable fubject for confinement, efpecially if his manner of living becomes more luxurious. Idlenefs brings on a redundency of the fluids, and a congeftion of that perfpirable matter, thrown off by exercife.

When this therefore is detained in the body, it will prove a ftimulus to many general and local difeafes. I have feen it verified in many inftances of gentlemen's horfes, who afford them leifure, and are not careful to apply that excellent fubftitute friction, or currying.

I now find a neceffity of changing my advice, and advocating the wretchednefs of thofe animals, whofe filent groans demand our commifferation.

Horfes cannot travel through heat and rain, over the fandy heath or rocky mountain, infenfible as the chariot to which he is harneffed. The rider fhould make his ftages, as the difficulty of the way and ftrength of the animal indicates. His limbs fhould be rubbed with a brufh or woolen cloth, to prevent their growing ftiff and fwelling; he fhould not be permitted to drink till cool
and

and in dusty weather his hay should be sprinkled with water, and his grain soaked at all seasons of the year. But these remarks will more properly occur, when I shall give directions for travelling horses.

All I need say further in this place is, consider what your beast is capable of performing, and the keeping you bestow on him; then require no more than reason exacts, and you may expect a long and faithful servant.

A REMARK OR TWO ON STABLES.

THE stabling of horses in the country, requires but few directions, their stables in general being capacious enough for a free circulation of air, which is as necessary for a horse, as for the human species. But where thirty or forty are kept together in a close stable, where the air has no access but by the door, together with the sharp exhalations from the urine, perspiration of their bodies, &c. it renders the situation disagreeable, and almost intollerable. A horse in health, to remain long in such a place, would soon be enervated and unfit for business. Stables should be situated where the air may have a draught through them; and in every horse's apartment a small window should be placed, and left open through the night, and not shut up to suffocate its inhabitants, as too frequently is the case in sea-port towns.

I shall now discourse upon the principal general disorders, to which horses are incident; next of local diseases, which will be connected with those of surgery. GLANDERS

GLANDERS or HORSE AIL.

THIS difeafe is juftly called the glanders, being principally an affection of the glands of the head; but from its frequent appearance, it is vulgarly called the horfe ail.

You will perceive this difeafe by the fadnefs of the horfe's countenance, lofs of appetite, difficulty in drinking, and fudden debility of ftrength. Frequently the glands under the jaws are fwelled, and in an advanced ftage of the difeafe, there will be a continual difcharge of thin ichorous matter from the nofe.

The remedies are thefe. Let blood freely in the mouth, or by perforating the nofe with a fharp awl; put him under a courfe of phyfic, by giving him brimftone, antimony and turmerick in fucceffion for two weeks. Let a dofe be given him every day in a mefs of bran. The dofe of brimftone and turmerick, half an ounce each; that of antimony, one fourth of an ounce. Put a rowel in his breaft, and then ftrive to bring the fwelling under his throat, to a fuppuration, by applying emolient poultices and fomenting paths. When the fwelling becomes foft, and the matter fluctuating, place a ceton in the moft depending part, to difcharge the humour. Fumigate his head twice a day, with fulphur and camphire mixed with rye pafte, dried, and burnt under his nofe; likewife fcraps of old leather—and occafionally blow fnuff up his nofe. If the difcharge of matter becomes thick, white and mild, you may foon expect a cure.

FRENZY

FRENZY or STAGGERS.

THIS difeafe is known by a hanging down of the head, watry eyes, and reeling of the body. From the general caufe of this difeafe, we infer the method of cure. The excretions are diminifhed, confequently a coftivenefs and induration of the contents of the inteftines, feems the caufe. The horfe muft be bled the firft day in the neck, the third day in the mouth; give him the firft day, four quarts of herb-drink, made of mallows and flax feed, to lubricate his bowels, and prepare for a dofe of aloes; one ounce and a half of which is to be given him the fecond day to purge him. The third day bleed in the mouth as before; the forth, give him tne following nourifhing decoction: Take two quarts of ale, boil in it a white loaf cruft, or hard bifcuit; when taken from the fire, add one gill of honey, and give it to the horfe luke-warm; put a plaifter of pitch upon his temples: Be fure to keep him in a dark ftable, and let his food be given him fparingly.

YELLOWS.

THIS difeafe in horfes is fimilar to the jaundice in men. It arifes from obftructions formed in the biliary ducts, which prevents the bile from flowing into the ftomach, but forces it to return into the circulation, which gives that yellow appearance in the whit of the eyes and urine, and that fenfe of wearinefs to the limbs in the animal difeafed.

CURE.

CURE.—Take aloes, venetian foap and honey equal quantities, to be made into pills, and half an ounce given daily for a week. If this does not effect a cure, fteep celandine and faffron in cyder, to be given one quart a day. It is often neceffary in this difeafe to let blood.

STRANGURY OR DIFFICULTY OF STALING.

MANY caufes may produce this difeafe, fuch as over fatigue or catching cold ; which brings on a ftricture in the renal veffels, and confequently an obftruction of urine. Another frequent caufe is, driving the beaft too long without fuffering him to ftop and ftale.

CURE.—Take one ounce of nitre and diffolve it in one quart of ale or beer, to be given the horfe blood warm ; or a pint of juniper berries boiled in two quarts of fair water to the confumption of one half, and given warm ; half an ounce of rofin pounded and given in meal a few days will perform wonders.

FEVER.

TO judge of the ftate of the fever, you may examine the pulfe ; which you will find in thin fkined horfes, by preffing your fingers gently on the temporal artery, about an inch and a quarter backward from the upper corner of the eye ; or in the infide of the leg, juft above the knee. But you may be better fatisfied by puting your hands to the horfe's noftrils, and judging from the heat of his breath.

CURE.—In the begining of a fever, it is generally neceffary to let blood, but in an advanced

B   ftate,

ftate, when the heat is great and the difcharge from the bowels diminifh*d*, or the dung hard and dry, glyfters are alfo neceffary.

For a glyfter or clyfter.

Take one handful of mallows, boil in milk and water, alfo two fpoonfuls of flax-feed; and add to it, when boiled, half a pound of fugar, and as much fweet oil, with a handful of falt; then with the neceffary apparatus, put it up the horfe's body.

You muft alfo obferve, a cooling regimen. Take a four pail pot and hang over your fire, full of water, and clover or honey-fuckle hay; make a tea of it. When your horfe is thirfty, let him drink it luke warm. Then take a quart of this liquor·and diffolve in it one ounce of nitre, to be given morning and evening, till the fever abates. Let his hay, if he will eat, be fprinkled with warm water, and his provender foaked.

CRAMP OR DRAWING OF THE NERVES.

THIS is a difeafe I have never read of, but have had many inftances of it in my practice. The almoft only caufe, is taking cold after hard labour and fweating. The excrefions being fuddenly diminifhed, brings on thefe fpafmodic and convulfive fymptoms. Upon the leaft motion, every nerve feems contracted, to overthrow its antagonift, and as it were to difmember its ungovernable body. The eyes are contorted in their fockets, and they are blind except by accident, and nothing but the white appears.

The

The method I have found of uncommon efficacy, is this. Immediately take a pound and half of blood from the jugular; then place your horse in a warm stable, and prepare to sweat him: Take a large pot, and fill it with May-weed and tansy; when boiled place it under the horse's belly, and cover, him with a large coverlet, to keep the steem of the bath confined to his body. A little previous to the bath, give him fifteen or eighteen grains of opium in half a pint of wine. Now take special care that the cold be not repeated; let him wear his covering a day or two, and carry him his water moderately warm. This meathod has proved salutary many times, and seems to have its reason in the nature of things.

———

HAVING attended briefly to the more general distempers, I shall call my reader's attention, to the more partial or local inconveniences, to which horses are subject. As I purpose brevity, I shall not enter into theoretical, or physical disputations on the subject, but strive to discover simple truth in a simple manner.

FISTULA.

THE fistula is an ulcer of the callous kind, and from its well known fatality to horses, is generally supposed incurable. I confess there are few diseases more stubborn, yet must remark, that neglect of means, or wrong applications have in ten instances to one, been the cause of my ill success. Its seat in horses is between the sadder and collar; which are commonly the source from

which

which it arifes. Bruifes of any kind may produce it. From its pofition on the top of the
withers, the matter when collected, inftead of
being difcharged, corrodes and infinuates between the cords of the neck, from which it can
hardily be eradicated. Moft people apply clay
mixed with vinegar, to the furface of the fore, to
dry it up; which might anfwer well, where a good
drain is opened; but here it proves a fource of
deception, and while you anticipate a cure, your
horfe is ruined.

My method of cure is this; firft with a limber
probe, fearch the bottom of the fore, fee whether
it is finuous or hollow; find the direction of the
finews, whether it runs between the fhoulder
blades, or only on one fide. When you have
made fufficient fearch into the depth of the fore,
and find it curable, you muft prepare to make a
drain from the bottom: and this muft be done
either by the knife or rowel.

Obfervation.—Where the rowel will anfwer,
never take the knife; for, by deftroying the te-
guments, you make a large fore, caufe great pain
to the beaft, and protract the cure. If roweling,
therefore, is propofed, make one of hair, put it
through the eye of a crooked needle; put your
needle to the bottom of the fore, and thruft it
through in a depending manner, that the difcharge
may be eafy; ftir it frequently, and wafh the fore
with ftrong lye, or foap fuds, to keep it clean.—
If fungous flefh arifes, fprinkle it with blue ftone,
or red precipitate: and fometimes fill the fore
with lime or afhes, which will help the digeftion,
and cleanfe the fore. If the fore is filled with a

callous

callous pipe, and appears of long standing; the knife or hot iron must be applied.

The horse being cast on an easy spot, with a knife or hot iron, as most convenient, you must take away the callous or fungous flesh, if it should bleed profusely, melt some rosin on the sore with a hot-iron, and sear the arteries. Lay a cloth upon the sore wet with spirit, and unbind your horse; if an inflamation succeeds, supple it with a hot bath, to reduce the swelling, and bring on a suppuration. Now, be careful to keep it from the air, and apply your digestive, made of basilicon; and if proud or fungous flesh is seen, add to it a little verdegrease. Yet, if after all your care, the matter falls between the shoulder-blades, or upon the neck bone, so that no drain can be made from the bottom of the sore; you had better give up the cure, and save your trouble.

Horses often have swellings upon their shoulders, that are not sinuous; in such cases, bathing with hot vinegar or urine will generally make a resolution of the humour, and prevent further mischief.

SHOULDER STRAIN.

THIS lameness is brought on by overstraining the limb. There is a collection of grumous blood, between the shoulder-blade and body; the small vessels being over-extended or ruptured by the strain, is the cause of that extravasated fluid, which must be re-absorbed or drained off, before the beast will get well.

CURE—My method of cure is this: Take up a piece of skin on the corner of the shoulder,

as

as large as a nine pence, then put your finger to the hole, and start the skin from the flesh two inches round, and blow up the shoulder. Now put in a piece of leather, cut round, with a hole in the middle, anfwering to that in the shoulder. This in about twelve or fifteen days, will discharge the humour, and being taken out, will seldom fail of a cure.

This method has been reprobated by fome; but experience has taught me to adopt it. Where the lamenefs is flight, I have found the following an efficacious remedy:

Take of high wines one pint, oil of fpike one gill, pigs' feet oil one gill, gum camphor half an ounce, and one beafts gall. Simmer thefe together over a gentle fire, apply it warm to the difeafed part, and heat it in with a difh of coals or hot flice twice a day.

CLAP IN THE BACK SINEWS.

THIS difeafe is a lamenefs in the back finews, between the knee and fetlock joint. It is produced by a ftrain, which debilitates the nerves, and therefore produces lamenefs. The cords of the leg will fometimes fwell, which will determine the feat of the difeafe; if not, you may know it from a fhoulder ftrain by the horfe's fteping fhort, but taking his foot from the ground; whereas, in a fhoulder ftrain, the horfe will, drag his toe on the ground when he walks.

CURE.——This may be eafily effected, by bathing the leg in the day time, with the ointment prefcribed for a fhoulder ftrain; at night apply an emollient poultice of turnips and indian meal.

Make

Make a boot for the horse's leg, tie it at the fetlock, then fill it with your poultice, and tie it again above the knee. This method followed a few days, will prove an efficacious remedy.

HIDE BOUND.

THIS is brought on by low keeping and surfeits; the juices of the body are dissipated, the skin becomes rigid, and as it were adheres to the ribs.——— To cure this inconvenience, it will be necessary to put your horse on a more liberal diet; also every day a mash of bran or boiled rye should be given him; and twice a week give him half an ounce of brimstone in his bran.

BROKEN WIND.

HORSES by over riding, especially when their bellies are full of water, or clover-hay, have their wind hurt, and are called broken-winded. The cure is difficult. Take of tar and honey one spoonful each; liquorish ball, half the quantity; opium, eight grains; mix and dissolve them in a quart of new milk, to be given every morning fasting. Let his water be that wherein quick lime has been slacked; the proportion is a pint of lime to a pail of water.

Feed him as much as possible on arse-smart hay, which has been sprinkled with warm water.

BOTS AND WORMS.

THE signs that indicate the botts, are uneasy motions in the horse, frequently turning his head to his sides, often lying down, or scouring of the guts. CURE.

CURE.---Sweeten one quart of milk with honey, and give it to the horse with a horn ; then powder half an ounce of aloes, and give it directly in a strong decoction of savine bows; if they have not eaten through the inteſtines, you may depend on a cure. Tobacco leaves cut fine, or coarſe horſe hair, and mixed with a horſe's provender, will prevent botts and worms from collecting in the maw ; and will often kill them.

GRIPES.

THIS diſeaſe hath ſimilar ſymptoms with the botts ; it ariſes from ſudden colds, indurated dung and ſpaſms of the inteſtines. If you are not ſure whether botts are the cauſe, take this method firſt, which will often deſtroy them :

Give the horſe three gills of gin, with as much ſweet oil ; if he is coſtive, give him an ounce of aloes, made into balls with caſtile ſoap and honey. If this does not work, give him a glyſter, made of tobacco-leaves ſteeped in old urine, and ſweetened with molaſſes ; theſe remedies are adapted as near as poſſible, to ſuit both diſorders.

SCOURING.

THIS is brought on by drinking too much cold water, or by eating ſour hay, &c.

CURE.---Give your horſe two quarts of the liquor, wherein garden rhubarb, flax-ſeed and mallows, have been boiled ; or boil white-oak bark, and white pine together ; give him one quart of this, morning and evening till well.

SORE

SORE BACK.

IF the skin is wore off a horse's back, and the sides of the sore are swelled, bath it with hot urine, or with salt and water; this will disperse the swelling. If you wish to dry up the sore, powder chalk, or old shoes burnt, and cover the sore with it. If his back is full of hard lumps, or what is commonly called saddle boils, bleed him freely in the mouth, which will serve as a dose of physic; then wash his back often with hot rum and vinegar.

BLEEDING.

THIS is a resourse which unskilful men fly to on every failure of their horse, without considering the nature of the disease, or state of the horse's body.

Proper subjects for bleeding.

HORSES that are affected with any inflamatory disorder, whether general or topical, as fevers, inflamed sores, or any hot humour, are proper subjects for bleeding. Horses that are fat and plethoric, require more frequent bleeding than those of the opposite state ; but observe not to deprive them of the vital fluid beyond necessity; rather bleed often, and but little at a time. Horses that are poor have no fluid to spare, rather recruit them by a generous diet and leisure.

Unskilful grooms, when they bleed in the jugular, often cut through the vein ; whence an extravasation of the blood, and no small danger to the horse.

Among many other instances, the Honorable *Benjamin Greenleaf*, Esq. sent me a horse in this condition.

condition. I ordered the servant to apply the simple remedy of cold water liberally, and in a few days he was cured.

PRICKED OR GRAVELED HOOFS.

HORSES are sometimes pricked in shoeing, it will fester, and cause the horse to be lame ; extract the nail and fill up the hole with the horse-ointment, to be mentioned by and by. Some times gravel will get into the nail hole or, into cracks in the hoof; unless this is soon extracted it will remain long in the hoof; and spoil the horse's use-fulness. Many by cutting the hoof to get out the gravel, make the remedy worse than the disease ; if you cannot find the gravel with a little cutting make a poultice of turnips and put the horse's foot into it, repeat this a few days, and the gravel will generally work out.

Note, if you omit this practice too long, the horse will not be cured till the gravel works out the top of the hoof.

The horse ointment.

Take yellow rosin, bees wax and honey like quantities ; hog's lard and turpentine, double their quantity ; melt them all together over a gentle fire, and keep a continual stiring : when they are well compounded, take it from the fire and stir in a little verdegrease.

This is an excellent ointment for sores, burns, bruises, chopped heels, &c.

SPAVINS.

THERE are three sorts of spavins. First, the bone spavin ; it is a bony excrescence formed on
the

the joint which impedes the motion of the joint and is feldom curable.

Secondly, the wind fpavin ; it commonly comes in the horfe's ham. Prick the fwelling with a phlegm knife, but take fpecial care not to injure the nervous cords, for this will often bring on th· lock jaw. Upon opening the fwelling, you will often find a gelatinous humour to iffue from the opening ; now apply your turnip poultice for a few days, to fuck out the humour ; then ftrengthen the part, by bathing it with good brandy.

Thirdly, the blood fpavin. The coats of the vein being ruptured, the blood extravafates and forms a protuberance in the vein.

CURE.—Take up the vein with a crooked needle, and tie it above the fwelling ; then let blood below it, and apply cow-dung fryed in goofe greafe and vinegar, by way of poultice.

SPLENT.

SPLENTS are of the fame nature with fpavins, but not upon the joints. They are bony excreffences of an oblong figure, coming between the fettock joint and knee, or gambrel ; while they are growing, they make the horfe lame, but when they are formed, unlefs they prefs upon the cords of the leg, they are of very little damage.

CURE.—Shave the part and put on a fmart bliftering plaifter, to be kept on three days ; chafe the part ftrongly with the tincture of flies ; and once a day rub in oppodeldoc with one quarter part oil of turpentine ; this will generally effect a cure, if curable.

WIND.

WIND GALLS.

THESE appear upon the fettocks, and are the confequence of hard riding. They are full of wind or jelly, they feldom lame a horfe, and may be cured in the fame manner that wind fpavins are.

RING-BONE.

THIS is a long callous juft above the hoof, if long neglected, the hoof will become narrow and twift, and often prove incurable.

I have cured many recent ring-bones in the following manner :---Make a boot for the horfe's foot, tie it at the top of the hoof, then take oyfter-fhell lime newly burned, and fill the boot againft the ring-bone with the lime ; place the horfe's foot in a tub of water, or in a pond of ftanding water ; repeat this five days ; after this poultice the foot for five days more with a turnip poultice and lin-feed oil ; obferving to chafe the part before you apply the poultice. Laftly apply a plaifter of pitch to the ring bone, to be worn two or three weeks. This method hath fucceeded with the greater half I have tried. Thofe who ufe ftone lime, may expect a fire that he cannot extinguifh, for by this, many have ruined their horfes.

SORE EYES.

IF the eyes are much inflamed, let blood in the neck, then boil the bark of bafs wood root with rofe leaves, fweeten the decoction with loaf fugar, wafh the horfes eyes three times a day with this water, and keep him in a dark ftable.

(as the wife man fays, in another cafe) train him up in the way he fhould go, and he will not forget it all his days.

A horfe is a tractable animal, and is fubjected to many fervile employments, when ufed with gentlenefs and good humour; yet they remember injuries, and have recollection to avoid appearances which once gave them pain. A horfe that ftumbles (and 'tis a good horfe that never ftumbles) if he is frequently chaftifed for it, will at the leaft miftep, exert himfelf to an uncommon degree, fearing the lafh, and often plunges himfelf and rider to the earth. This conduct muft arife from the remembrance of his ftripes, on fimilar occafions.

If your horfe efpies an object of fear in his way, heighten not the fenfation with a whip or harfh words; for he will prefently imagine them all connected, and double his flight. Gentlemen who intend a horfe for the carriage, fhould familiarife him to the harnefs in fome coach or waggon, where he cannot get away, till he fubmits himfelf tamely to be checked and forwarded at pleafure.

I now think it proper to give a few directions relative to docking, nicking, &c.

The curtailing of horfes is both ornamental and ufeful; a long tail, if the roads are muddy gathers much dirt, and impedes the horfe's travelling. Many horfes of worth make but little figure on account of their low carriage; the elevation of the tail therefore, is the object of enquiry. For this purpofe the horfe fhould be caft on fome eafy fpot, that you may act with caution, then

place

place a block under the tail, and hold your dividing inftrument obliquely, fo as to cut the under finews the fhorteft; then their antagonifts acting with fuperior force, will elevate the tail. Should the arteries bleed profufely, feal them with a hot iron, and anoint the fore every day with fome emolient ointment, till it is well.

If nicking is thought neceffary, the horfe muft be caft as for docking: the apparatus being ready, which fhould be a phlegm knife, a fmall pair of pincers, an iron fpatula, and a cup of warm fpirits: then with your knife, make an incifion upon the cord of the tail which lies on each fide of the bone, one inch and half long, four inches from the body; the cord appearing take hold of it with your pincers and run the fpatula under it, then cut the cord at the upper part of the incifion next the body, and do the fame by the other cord. Then at two inches from your former incifion, towards the end of the tail, cut down upon the cords as before, and take away four inches of each cord, or if it is thought neceffary, the whole of the cord may be taken away in the fame manner. Now apply your fpirit, and bind up the fore with a linnen bandage; unbind the horfe and put him into a very narrow ftable, fix a pulley over his back, put a line through and tie one end to the horfe's tail, with a fufficient weight on the other end, to keep the tail upright; wet it daily with fpirit, and apply fome digeftive, fuch as bafilicon, and in ten or fifteen days, you may expect a cure.

OBSER-

OBSERVATIONS ON PRESERVING HEALTH.

HEALTH, is that ſtate of an animal body, in which all the functions relative thereto, are performed with eaſe and agility; the food received, is duly aſſimulated to the nouriſhment of the body, the fluids have a free, and equable round of circulation, and the fibres or nervous ſyſtem, which is accounted the ſpring of ſenſation and motion, are not become rigid and inelaſtic; which would give riſe to every ſpecies of inflamitory affection; neither flaxed, lax or weak, which would indulge a decline, and ſoon put a period to his exiſtence.

In order therefore, to ſecure a horſe in a ſtate of health, and prevent a train of ills, we muſt have a ſpecial regard to him, with reſpect to food, exerciſe and ſtabling.

The intent of this treatiſe is, not to loſe ſight of the main object, while we are buſying with unneceſſary details—thoſe who are fond of prolixity, may conſult Clark's Farrier on the ſubject.

I ſhall now lay before my readers, the ſeveral ſorts of ſodder and grain, uſed for horſes, with the choice of each.

The principal hay for horſes, is herd-graſs and clover: the grain, oats, rye, barley, corn, bran, potatoes, &c. Some farmers, indeed, can ſupport their horſes on meadow or ſalt hay; but I preſume, unleſs grain is ſubſtituted for better ſodder, ſuch horſes are unfit for daily and laborious exerciſe; and if required, ten to one, he quits the ſervile ſcene, and leaves May verdant hill for happier brutes.   Herd-

Herd-grass if well made, is the best fodder; it is more nutritious according to its weight than clover. Horses however are extremely fond of clover, and it keeps the bowels loose, but if indulged their fill, and immediately put to exercise, it may be of bad consequence, and often bring on what is called the phthisic. Farmers frequently feed their horses through the winter on corn fodder; it is very good if rightly managed.

A horse is an animal of a hot constitution, and especially when fed on dry meat, is subject to costiveness—this should be guarded against by gentle laxatives. A mess of potatoes every day, or a mash of bran, or boiled rye, will generally keep the bowels loose, and secure your horse from those complaints, which counterfeit the bots, or another disorder which is called the dry belly-ache. Oats, the common provender for horses in our country, contain a latent spirit which supports the beast under great fatigue, and encourages them to the most servile employment with the greatest freedom; yet if a small portion of corn should be added to every feed of oats, they would probably be broken much finer, and consequently be more nutritious. Barley is also very grateful to horses, but much the best ground. In feeding your horses, whether you serve up the hay in a manger or rack, be careful to give no more than your horse will eat with a good appetite; lest suffering to breathe upon, and spoil the sweetness of his hay, you imagine him sick, and either send him to the Farrier, or take some method with him, that will make him truly sick. Give

If films grow over the eye, diſſolve ten grains of white vitriol and as much rock allum in a gill of ſpring water, dip a feather into it, and touch the eye a few days with it, and it will eat away the film.

SCRATCHES.

HORSES are troubled with theſe moſt frequently in the ſpring, while the roads are muddy, which obſtruĉts the perſpiration of the parts ; together with the ſnow-water, which is very unfavourable to this diſorder.

CURE.—Cut the hair off. cloſe, and waſh the legs with ſtrong ſoap ſuds or urine ; put on a turnip-poultice (as this is the beſt I know of for horſes) a few days, mixed with hog's fat and linſeed oil ; it will ſoon effeĉt the cure.

FILING TEETH.

WHEN horſes are old, their fore-teeth grow long, while their jaw-teeth wear ſhort ; this prevents the horſes from grinding their hay ; and by that means they grow poor and die, before their natural vigour is exhauſted. To remedy this inconvenience, and prolong a ſerviceable life, provide a gag to put in his mouth, then a coarſe file—having gaged your horſe, file his fore teeth ſo ſhort that his grinders may touch, and break the hardeſt hay.

This is an eaſy and certain method of making old horſes eat their hay equal to young ones ; provided their jaw-teeth are ſound.

C   STIFLE.

STIFLE.

THE ſtifle joint is above the inſide bend of the hough or gambrel; its uſe is much the ſame as the knee-pan in man. If the ſtifle is only ſtrained, bath it with the ointment preſcribed for ſtrains in the hip; which will ſoon cure it. If it is diſlocated, or out of place, make a ſtifle ſhoe, in form of a cone—let a natural ſhoe be the baſe; then with three pieces of iron, one from the toe, the other two from the ſides of the ſhoe, to meet in a point three inches from the baſe. Put this upon the well foot, that the horſe may ſtand upon the lame one four or five days; that will keep the joint in place---and in the mean time bath the part with the ointment above mentioned. Note---The ſtifle ſhoe is preferable to ſtraping the well leg, for ſtraping hinders the circulation, brings off the hair, and often lames the well leg.

STRAINS IN THE HIP.

HORSES are frequently lame in the hip; this is occaſioned by the ligament which holds the thigh bone into the ſocket, being overſtretched. To effect a cure, the horſe muſt have but little exerciſe, and the joints ſhould be bathed three times a day, with three parts of brandy, and one of oil of ſpike to be heat in by a chafing-diſh of coals; this will contract and ſtrengthen the ligament, and if a recent lameneſs, will prove a certain remedy.

HIPED AND HALF HIPED.

WHEN the bones of the hip fall fo low as to be called hiped, the horfe becomes ufelefs; but when they are only half hiped, or hip-fhot, the hip may be ftrengthened, and the horfe (though dif-figured) may perform much labour.

CURE——Take white-oak bark, elm and white-pine bark; roots, Solomon-feal, buck horn and comfrey; boil them all together, and frequently bath the hip with it: this in a little time will ftrengthen the hip and fit the horfe for bufinefs.

HOOF BOUND.

HOOFS that are hard, dry, and withal con-tracted at the top fo as to pinch upon the quick, and prevent a free circulation, are faid to be hoof bound. To prevent this, keep the hoofs cool and moift; to cure it, take a phlegm lancet, and open the hoof at the edge of the hair, to give it liberty of fpreading. Then greafe it daily with woodchuck, fkunk or dog's greafe, that it may grow.

A few directions for chufing a HORSE.

THERE is much pleafure and profit in the fervice of a good horfe, but very little of either in a bad one. There are many mean horfes that make a good appearance when taken from the hand of a jockey. In purchafing a horfe, then, truft not too much to the feller's word; let your own judgment, or that of a friend, be chiefly re-lied on. See that he hath good feet and joints, and that he ftands well on his legs; fee that his fore-teeth fhut even, for many horfes have their

under

under jaw the ſhorteſt; theſe will grow poor at graſs. See that his hair is ſhort and fine, for this denotes a good horſe. Obſerve his eyes, that they are clear and free from blemiſhes, that they are not moon eyed, or white eyed, for ſuch are apt to ſtart in the night. A large hazel coloured eye is the beſt.

Look at his knees, ſee that the hair or ſkin is not broken, for this denotes a ſtumbler. Take care that his wind is good; for a trial of this, let him be fed on good hay for twenty-four hours, take him then to water, and let him drink his fill; place him with his head the loweſt, if then he will breathe free, there is no danger. See that his countenance is bright and cheerful; this is an excellent mirror to diſcover his goodneſs in. If his noſtrils are broad, it is a ſign that he is well winded; narrow noſtrils the contrary.

See that his ſpirits are good, but that he is gentle and eaſily governed, not inclined to ſtart.—In travelling, mind that he lifts his feet neither too high or too low: that he does not interfere or overreach, and that he carries his hind legs the wideſt. See that he is well rib'd back, and not high boned. The ſize may be determined by the purchaſer. Age, from five to ten is the beſt. There are many tricks practiſed by jockies, to make horſes appear young, but it is not conſiſtent with the ſize of my book, to detect them; all I would ſay is, that horſes teeth when young, are wide, white and even; the inſide of their mouths are fleſhy, and their lips hard and firm. On the contrary, the mouth of an old horſe is lean above and below, the lips are ſoft and eafily turned up; their teeth grow longer narrower, and of a yellow colour.

REMARKS ON TRAVELLING.

ACCORDING to my promife, I fhall give my readers a few directions relative to travelling horfes. If you are to take a long journey, you muft prepare your horfe by good feeding and gentle exercife. A horfe that is exhaufted with hard labour, advanced in age, or very young, will not bear the fatigues of a long journey—Neither will a very fat horfe, or one who has lived without exercife, be a fit fubject for travelling. A horfe, therefore, rather meager than fat, ufed to active exercife, whofe flefh is firm from good living and labour, is the moft likely to anfwer your expectation. Some days before your journey, have him fhod, left being pricked with a nail, he fail you on the road. Look well to the faddle, and fee it fits with cafe, and does not gall his back; and while upon the road examine it daily, and repair it as needed.

Before your horfe eats in the morning, give him a little water, that he may eat the better; but do not lead him to the trough or brook till you take him out for riding; the water now taken into the ftomach, will better dilute the food; and by wafhing his mouth, prevent any fudden thirft on the road. Ride moderately while your horfe's belly is full, for he will mend his pace as this fulnefs goes off.

Before you make a ftage, reftrain your horfe, and take him in cool; let him eat a little hay before he is watered, if hot; and thus conduct at

all

all your stages. At night, after your horse is cooled, wash his legs with water, (warm water is best) for it promotes perspiration, cleanses away the sand, and prevents his legs from swelling. His back should likewise be washed, to prevent those little saddle boils which the friction of the saddle often produces. In the middle of the day, I should prefer a bating of hay to any grain; but let it be sprinkled in warm weather with water. New oats are not good for a horse, on a journey; they make him faint, and often bring on a diarkea. If old oats cannot be had (as is sometimes the case at harvest) feed him with indian meal, or oat meal. Horses on a journey, from their increased perspiration, and constant feeding on dry meat, are apt to be costive; to prevent this, give them occasionally a marsh of bran, or boiled rye.

If your horse discovers an inclination to ☐ on the road, let him stop for that purpose; if the discharge is difficult, give him an ounce ☐ ☐tre for a few nights in his provender. A ho☐ ☐ath not the faculty of speech, but subjects hi☐elf to his master, to whom he complains under every indisposition. Will not then reason, interest, and pity, prompt us to adopt the most approved methods for their welfare?

PART ·

Of the DISEASES of CATTLE.

CATTLE are subject to many diseases, at all seasons of the year, but more especially in the spring ; which I shall endeavour in a brief manner to give an account of.

FEVER.

WHEN a fever takes place, the beast loses his appetite, the nose becomes dry, and the horns cold, the eyes appear dull and the countenance fallen.

In the beginning of the disease, one quart of blood should be taken from the jugular ; but if the fever is far advanced, and a trembling or ing of the muscles has taken place, to bleed be dangerous, and often fatal. Boil fever-bush and angelica, like quantities ; give the beast one gallon at a time twice a day, also one gill of sweet oil per day. The above dose is for an ox or cow ; for lesser cattle, it must be in proportion.

MURRAIN.

THIS disorder comes under the nether jaw, the chaps swell, and upon search you find it full of a watery humour. This disease commonly happens to cattle that are thin of flesh.

CURE.—

CURE.—In the firſt place put a rowel thro' the moſt depending part of the ſwelling, to be ſtired frequently, then give the beaſt the following ſingular, but eſſicacious remedy.

Take half a pint of hen's dung and diſſolve in one quart of old urine, and cauſe the beaſt to drink it. This, if applied ſeaſonably, will never fail of a cure.

COUGH OR SHORTNESS OF BREATH.

CURE.—Give the beaſt to drink divers mornings together, one ſpoonful of tar, and as much honey, diſſolved in a quart of new milk, with one head of garlick bruiſed, and put in with it.

WIND CHOLIG.

THIS is diſcovered by the beaſt being very uneaſy, lying down and getting up often, and frequent ſwelling very much.

CURE.—Take a quart of warm water and a pint of gin, ſweetened well with molaſſes, then put in half a pint of pounded muſtard ſeed, pour it down, and drive the beaſt about and it will move the wind.

FOR THE SCAB OR SCURF.

TAKE ſoft ſoap and tar and anoint the place, and it will ſoon cure it.

FOR PISSING OF BLOOD.

TAKE milk and bring it to a curd with runnet, mix it with aſh leaves and nettle ſeeds choped fine, and made into balls, to be put down the beaſt's throat.   BLADDERS.

BLADDERS.

THIS difeafe happens under the tongue, being a number of fmall bladders, full of a watery humour : the beaft breathes with difficulty and drools at the mouth.

CURE.—The faline watery humour muft be let out with an incifion knife, or the bladders may be broken with your fingers. Then give the beaft water to drink wherein bay falt and bay leaves have been concocted.

TAINT OR GARGET.

THIS is a hot humour that moftly affects cows bags, but fome times their limbs, and other cattle alfo.

CURE.—If the humour affects the cow's bag, the firft thing to be done, is to take two pounds of blood from the neck, then put a piece of garget root in the double fkin between the fore legs with a hair rowel below that ; when the humour fubfides take the garget and rowel out, wafh the bag three or four times a day with cold brine. If the fwelling increafes, fcarify the fkin and wafh it with the brine of falt and urine.

If the garget affects the limbs, after bleeding, you muft make a tea of horfe-readifh root, muftard feed and fage ; give the beaft two quarts at a time, daily, till well.

BLAINS.

THIS is a ftoppage of the body, attended with a fever. It hath all the fymptoms of fever, fuch as dry nofe, cold horns, &c. The body fwells, and they make conftant efforts to dung but difcharge little.

CURE.

CURE.—Take away one quart of blood; then let some person skilled in the business, put his hand into the creature's body after it is well greased, and take away the indurated dung; then such things as are physical must be given. First take one quart of chamber-lye, half a pint of molasses with as much hogs-lard, let them be simered together, then add a spoonful of gun-powder pounded, let it be put down the creature's throat with a horn. If the fever is not high, Hiera Picra is a good medicine, and the herb thoroughwort made into a strong tea will often effect a cure.

FOR ANY POISONOUS THING EATEN.

TAKE milk, sallad oil and london treacle, mix them together and give warm.

TO KILL WORMS

TAKE savine, cut it fine and make it into balls, with fresh butter, to be put down the creature's throat. Or give half an ounce of powdered aloes in a quart of savine tea.

HORN AIL.

THIS disease is seated in the horns of cattle, the inside becomes carious, putrefies and is discharged from the nose. The beast that is taken with this disorder will frequently shake his head, and appear to be dizzy. If you would be sure of this disease, take a nail gimlet and perforate the horn, if it is hallow and no blood follows, it is the horn ail.

CURE.—Bore each horn into the hollow part, then inject into it strong vinegar and camphorated ed spirits; this will cleanse the horn and generally effect the cure.

OVER FLOWING OF THE GALL.

THIS distemper is similar to the jaundice in men or the yellows in horses. The beasts grow suddenly weak, eat but little, often have a cough, their eyes and urine turn yellow.

CURE.—Any thing bitter is good, cherry-tree bark, barberry bark, of celandine steeped in cyder will generally effect a cure.

CATTLE's TEETH THAT ARE LOOSE.

CURE.—Rub their teeth well with fine salt, and it will fasten them.

BARBS IN THE MOUTH.

THESE are little white protuberances growing on the inside of the cheeks. In their natural state they are about one third of an inch long, but when they grow to such a length as to get between the teeth and turn blue, the beast will not eat, but grows poor and slavers at the mouth.

CURE.—Cut the barbs with a pair of scissors, and rub them with fine salt, which will soon cure them.

TO STOP VOMITING.

BOIL tansy and mint together; give one quart of this to the beast. If it does not stop in an hour, give the same quantity again, and repeat it till stopped.

FOR LOSS OF THE CUD.

WHEN cattle lose the cud, they will not masticate their food the second time, as they usually do; neither will they eat with an appetite.

CURE.---

CURE.—The quickeſt and beſt method is to take half the cud from another creature, and put it warm into the mouth of that which hath loſt it; this remedy is infallible.

TO CURE WENS.

WENS, except thoſe that are ſitfaſts, are eaſily cured. When they appear to be ripe, put a hair rowel through the middle of them, and put on daily, ſoft ſoap.

BROKEN HORNS.

CATTLE, by many accidents, may have their horns broken, and unleſs proper methods are taken with them, they eithe r loſe their horns, or have them grow in a very unnatural manner.

CURE.—If they are not broken ſo as to come off from the frith, or even if they are, I have often-cured them, by replacing them quickly, and making uſe of the following method.—Take a piece of wood and put acroſs the horns to keep them their uſual width; then put another piece in the middle of the former, to reſt upon the forehead, bringing the horns in their natural poſition: laſtly, prepare a bandage two or three yards long, four inches wide, to be dipped in facing pitch, while warm; when this is cold, it will keep the horn very firm, and being left on for three or four weeks, it will get perfectly well.

BROKEN LEGS.

THE farther a leg is broken from the joint, the better; fractures in the hip are ſeldom cured.

CURE.—Take ſolomon ſeal root, buck horn and comfrey roots, each a handful, to be boiled

in

in tar for a knitting plaſter to be placed next the leg; then ſplinter it in the proper place, and with your narrow bandage bind it up, let it remain till it is well. It is ſometimes neceſſary to ſling the beaſt, that he may not miſplace the leg by ſtanding.

TAPING.

WHEN catlſe are ſwelled very much, it is often neceſſary to reduce them by taping. Take a ſharp knife, gage it about an inch, and pierce the belly of the beaſt juſt below the ſhort ribs (always on the left ſide) then either keep the knife in and preſs it ſideways, or put in a quill that the wind may extricate itſelf.

FALLING DOWN OF THE MATRICE OR REED.

COWS juſt before or after calving, if they are weak and ſuffered to lie with their hinder parts the loweſt, ſometimes have their reed protruded or inverted. When this has happened and the part is ſwelled or torn (for hens will pick and tear it to pieces, if they are ſuffered to) waſh it with warm milk and water, to cleanſe it of the filth and dirt; then boil a ſtrong decoction of white oak or ſome other aſtringent bark, and bath the part till it is contracted ſo as to be replaced in the body. Give the cow half a pint of brandy with a nutmeg grated in it as a cordial, prepare her beding ſo that her hinder parts may lay the higheſt, and ring her up with three ſtrong-wire-rings.

CALVING.

COWS fometimes need affiftance to bring forth their young; if they have ftrength, the fituation of the calf may make it difficult, if not impracticable. Naturally a calf prefents its fore feet and head firft; but if this is the cafe, and the head of the calf is fallen below the bones, the hand muft be introduced into the body, and pufh the calf back, and withal rafe his head above the bones, then he may be taken away with eafe. If the calf fhould be inverted and prefent his tail firft, the hand fhould be put into the cow's body and the calf turned if poffible. If that cannot be done, you may indeavour to bring it away by the hind legs, which may be done many times with eafe. The cow fhould ftand if fhe hath ftrength, which will greatly facilitate the delivery. The fecundine or cleanfing fhould be taken away directly after the calf, for if fuffered to remain long in the body, it is attended with many bad confequences.

PERFORATING COWS DUGS.

IT fometimes happens that cows when they calve, have their dugs knotted, and the paffage through them becomes impervious, they confequently give no milk. To remedy this inconvenience, make a fmall fkewer of walnut or whalebone, and force it up the middle of the dug; take it out daily and anoint it with goofe greafe, do thus till it heals round the fkewer. I have been fuccefsful in many attempts of this kind, and would recommend it as the beft method, in cafes of this fort.

CALVES THAT SCOUR.

YOUNG calves are fubject to a loofenefs or fcouring.

CURE.—Take a pint of new milk, and put two fpoonfuls of runnet into it; to be put immediately down the calves ftomach, this forming a curd in the ftomach, will prevent the flux.

CATTLE THAT ARE OVERHEAT.

I HAVE frequently feen cattle, efpecially oxen, that from too much fatigue in hot weather, were what fome call melted, or overheat. This brings on fuch a relaxed ftate of the folids, that nature will feldom reftore them to their primitive tone. The circulation, being impeded (which always fucceeds overheating) confequently the perfpiration is diminifhed and retained, and the beaft remains an inactive drone for life.

CURE.—Give the beaft directly one quart of gin, or for want of that W. India rum, this acting as a ftimulus, will ftrengthen the folids, quicken the fluids, promote all the fecretions, and very generally effect a cure.

TAIL SICK.

CATTLE in the fpring feafon, more efpecially young ones, are what is commonly called tailfick. The end of the tail for fome inches becomes loofe and fpongy, the creature lofes its appetite, and fick. The fimple remedy is, cut off the tail above the loofe part, and it will form a cure.

BLEEDING.

THE beſt time to bleed is the ſpring of the year and increaſe of the moon. Old cattle require oftener bleeding than young ones; but the quantity ſhould be leſs. Cattle you intend to fat, ſhould be bled three or four months ſucceſſively, in the firſt part of the year, in the increaſe of the moon, and but little at a time. In all other caſes you muſt bleed as the exigencies of the caſe require, and as metioned in the various diſeaſes.

PART

PART III

Of SHEEP.

A SHEEP perhaps, is one of the most useful animals of our country; their annual fleece being manufactured at home, or in our now flourishing woolen-manufactories, afford us a neat and comfortable apparel; their flesh a wholsome food for our tables.

Sheep are of a hot nature, and require to be kept cool, they should not be housed, except in rainy weather. Ewes before they lamb, should have corn, beans, or turnips every day, which will enable them to bring forth their young with vigour. After they have lambed, a few potatoes every day will make a flow of milk; if they should bring on a loosenefs, give them corn instead of potatoes.

Sheep should be sheared, the moon increasing, their wool will be longer and better; some shear their lambs in August, affirming that the succeeding fleece is not the less for it. Sheep should be washed in the spring with a decoction of tobacco; this will kill the ticks, and prevent their rubbing the wool off.

I shall now enumerate some of the malad ies to whis sheep are subject.

PLAGUE.

PLAGUE.

WASH the sheep in allum and salt water, and give them to drink a decoction of rue and balm leaves.

TO CURE POISON.

WHEN snow falls before you have taken up your sheep, they often, through force of hunger, eat winter-green, which will make them froth at the mouth and swell, and in a little time die.

CURE.—Take a gill of sweet oil, or for want of that hogs-fat or fresh butter ; mix it with a pint of new milk to be given to the sheep; if it is taken seasonably it will effect the cure.

LOSS OF THE CUD.

TAKE the cud from another sheep and divide it betwixt the two, or mix clay in urine with the powder of allum, make it up in little balls and put one or two down the sheeps throat, and after it half a pint of vinegar.

TO INCREASE MILK.

IN the spring give the ewes beans, corn, or potatoes, and in the summer change of pasture, this will increase the milk, and make the lambs to grow well.

FOR THE SCAB OR ITCH.

ANOINT the part affected with tar and fresh butter mixed together, or wash the sheep in pennyroyal water, and it will preserve them from the scab.

FEVER.

FEVER IN SHEEP.

DISSOLVE half an ounce of nitre in water and vinegar, and give it to the sheep luke-warm.

TO KILL MAGGOTS IN SHEEP.

MIX tar and goose greafe, equal quantities, and ftir in flower of fulpher, as much as to make it of a proper confiftence, anoint the place with the ointment, and it will kill them.

FOR A COUGH.

TAKE colts-foot, lung-wort, and maiden hair, boil them to a ftrong tea, fweeten it with honey, and give it the fheep to drink.

FOR THE STAGGERS.

DISSOLVE affafœtida in warm water, and put half a fpoonful in each ear of the fheep—It is a fpeedy remedy.

TO PRESERVE FROM THE ROT.

TAKE the falt that is gathered from the marfhes in fummer, or for want of that, falt and allum; rub the mouth of the fheep with this once a week, and it will preferve them from the rot.

PART.

PART IV.

Of DISEASES in SWINE.

A HOG is a very bad creature to doctor, there=
fore, to prevent their difeafes, fhould be an object of
our attention.

Keep him well if you can, but not fo as to bur-
den him with fat in hot weather; keep his body
open, and there will be little danger of his being
fick. Brimftone, in fmall dofes, is excellent for
a hog; antimony is alfo good; but if you can
get neither, chamber lie put in their fwill, will
anfwer a good purpofe. It is neceffary to keep
a hog's iffues open; but I fhall make fome remarks
upon this elfewhere. The practice of feeding
ftore hogs three times a day, is not good; whereas
if they are fed only morning and night, they keep
their appetite, eat their food clean, and grow the
fafter.

I fhall now fay a few things on the difeafes of
hogs.

MEASLES IN SWINE.

RUB them all over with a ftiff brufh dipped in
cold water, then boil parfley-roots and rue in falt
water, and give it them to drink.

FOR

FOR A FEVER.

LET them blood in the tail, and give them thrice a day, water wherein pepper and parfnip-roots have been bolied.

FOR THE SWINE POX.

TAKE an ounce of nitre, pound it, and diffolve it in a point of cyder; add to it half a pint of fweet oil and one fpoonful of honey, to be given to the fwine luke-warm.

FOR CATARRHS.

TAKE two ounces of coriander-feed, one of ginger, three of honey, and half an ounce of turmeric, let it be powdered fine and boiled in three quarts of new milk, then let the hog drink it.

OF DRENCHES.

IT is a practice among people in general, when their hogs are fick, to put a rope in their mouths and hang them up to drenching. This is a very bad practice—for while you are pouring your medicine down, the hog will fqeak, and ten to on the liquid goes down the wind pipe and choaks him. If you can give your hog his medicine in milk, or fome other food, that he will drink, it is well; if not, do not force it down in the manner of drenching, but give it to him in the form of a glyfter: This is always fafe and as effectual as any method whatever.

ISSUES.

THE iffues in a hog, are places on the infide of their legs, which are porous, like a pepperbox top. Here it feems, is the moft immediate outlet for the fuperfluous fluid of the body, when thefe get ftopped (as hogs are fond of filth and mire) the hog lofes his appetite, and becomes fick ; then to drenching and choaking as before hinted ; whereas if his iffues were rubbed and picked open he would immediately recover.

Thus I have endeavoured in the preceeding fheets, with much brevity and plainnefs, to treat upon thofe maladies, which have fallen more immediately under my infpection. I would not be thought a plagiary. I have made practical experince my guide, without regard to ftudied theories ; I have not, however, difcarded the fentiments of any man, becaufe they agreed with my own ; and if they may be in any meafure ferviceable to my readers, I fhall **never regret** my trouble in writing them.

FIRST PART.

THIRD PART.

FOURTH PART.